SUPER TURBO

MEETS THE CAT-NAPPERS

By Lee Kirby
Illustrated by George O'Connor

LITTLE SIMON

New York   London   Toronto   Sydney   New Delhi

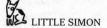 LITTLE SIMON

An imprint of Simon & Schuster Children's Publishing Division • 1230 Avenue of the Americas, New York, New York 10020 • First Little Simon paperback edition July 2018. Copyright © 2018 by Simon & Schuster, Inc. All rights reserved, including the right of reproduction in whole or in part in any form. LITTLE SIMON is a registered trademark of Simon & Schuster, Inc., and associated colophon is a trademark of Simon & Schuster, Inc. For information about special discounts for bulk purchases, please contact Simon & Schuster Special Sales at 1-866-506-1949 or business@simonandschuster.com. The Simon & Schuster Speakers Bureau can bring authors to your live event. For more information or to book an event contact the Simon & Schuster Speakers Bureau at 1-866-248-3049 or visit our website at www.simonspeakers.com. Designed by Jay Colvin. The text of this book was set in Little Simon Gazette.
Manufactured in the United States of America 0618 MTN 10 9 8 7 6 5 4 3 2 1
Cataloging-in-Publication Data for this title is available from the Library of Congress.
ISBN 978-1-5344-1185-2 (hc)
ISBN 978-1-5344-1184-5 (pbk)
ISBN 978-1-5344-1186-9 (eBook)

CONTENTS

1

A BIG ANNOUNCEMENT

But right now, lunch was more important than some big secret. Every human from Classroom C was in the cafeteria, eating their bologna sandwiches or grapes or hummus or whatever it was they had brought from home for lunch. For the kids who were buying their

lunch, today's special was a "meat surprise." Too bad for those kids.

Now, it's true that every *human* from Classroom C was having lunch in the cafeteria. But that doesn't mean every*one* from Classroom C was there. This is Turbo, the official pet of Classroom C, and as you can see, he is no human.

HE'S A HAMSTER. DUH!

Turbo was taking his lunch as he always did, sitting in his comfy cage surrounded by cedar chips, admiring his shiny, squeaky hamster wheel and looking out onto his classroom. Turbo loved being the official pet of Classroom C. But he also loved lunchtime, when he was alone in the classroom. It was the only part of the school day when he could relax and not have to pretend he was just an average, ordinary hamster.

That brings us back to the big secret. You see, Turbo wasn't average and ordinary because he was actually . . .

SUPER GOGGLES!

SUPER CAPE!

CUTE FUZZY EARS!

TWITCHY PINK NOSE!

ABLE TO FLY!

As Super Turbo finished his hamster pellets, the bell rang to signal that lunch was over for the humans, too.

"Well, back to work!" said Turbo to no one in particular. He hopped on his hamster wheel and began to run, just like an average, ordinary hamster would.

As the students of Classroom C filed

back into the room, many of them walked by Turbo's cage to wave hi. Turbo squeaked a little hamster squeak at each of them. The kids loved Turbo, and he loved them.

Ms. Beasley, the second-grade teacher, took her place in the front of her room and cleared her throat. "Listen up, class, I have an announcement!"

Turbo's ears perked up. An announcement from Ms. Beasley could mean a lot of things. It could mean the class was having a pop quiz. Turbo always felt bad for them when that happened. Or it could mean they were getting a water fountain that was for chocolate milk instead of water! Or it could mean something . . . evil. And Turbo *always* had to be prepared for evil.

"As you know," said Ms. Beasley, "we have a holiday weekend coming up. And that means one of you will have an important assignment."

The class started whispering with excitement.

This doesn't sound evil so far, thought Turbo.

"Now, normally I'd take Turbo home with me for the long weekend. But I'm headed out of town, and I bet Turbo could use a vacation from these linoleum halls too. So, anyone who wants to take Turbo home, ask your parents' permission tonight and you can put your name in a hat on Friday."

The class buzzed excitedly at this news.

Turbo sat down in his cage. A trip home with a student! Turbo had

done this before, and he wondered whose house he'd be visiting this time. Well, one thing was sure. No matter who Turbo went home with, it was going to be an adventure!

SUPERPETS, ASSEMBLE!

Super Turbo paced back and forth in the book nook of Classroom C, waiting for the rest of the Superpet Superhero League to arrive.

Wait, what's that? You don't know about the Superpet Super-hero League? You don't know about how they have saved Sunnyview

Elementary, and even the world, more times than you could count on…four fingers?

Well, here they come now. Meet the team.

FIRST UP IS ANGELINA, AKA WONDER PIG. SHE HAS AN EXCELLENT SENSE OF DIRECTION. SHE ALSO HAS SUPER-PIG STRENGTH.

AND CLEVER, THE GREEN WINGER. OBVIOUSLY, THE GREEN WINGER CAN FLY, BUT SHE CAN ALSO DO LOTS OF COOL ACROBATICS!

THIS IS FRANK, AKA BOSS BUNNY. HIS CUTE BUNNY NOSE CAN SNIFF OUT TROUBLE, AND HIS UTILITY BELT CAN GET HIM OUT OF ANY JAM!

AND FINALLY, HERE'S WARREN, AKA PROFESSOR TURTLE. PROFESSOR TURTLE IS SLOW BUT SUPER SMART.

OH, WAIT! CAN'T FORGET PENELOPE. SHE DOESN'T HAVE A SUPERHERO NAME YET, BUT SHE'S A CHAMELEON, SO SHE CAN CHANGE COLORS. THAT'S PRETTY SUPER!

The Great Gecko stood behind a stack of books and called the Super-pet Superhero League meeting to order.

The Great Gecko blinked in surprise. "Okay, wow! Well, who wants to go first?" he asked.

"It's a holiday weekend and I'm going home with a student!" blurted out Super Turbo . . . and Wonder Pig . . . and the Green Winger, all at the same time.

The Green Winger was the official classroom pet of Classroom D. She explained, "My kids are having a reading contest, and the one who reads the most books gets to take me home for the holiday weekend."

"For me, it's the kid who does the best job coloring in the lines," said Wonder Pig. She was the official pet of Classroom B, which was a first-grade classroom.

"My kids are all putting their names in a hat . . . whatever that means," Turbo offered.

BUT WHAT ABOUT YOU OTHER GUYS?

WELL, I'LL BE GOING HOME WITH PRINCIPAL BRICKFORD, LIKE I USUALLY DO. HE'S A BIG FAN.

ANYWAYS, WE SCALY GUYS DON'T NEED TO EAT AS MUCH AS YOU FUZZY GUYS DO. I'M STILL FULL FROM LAST WEEK!

AND BESIDES, WHILE YOU GUYS ARE AWAY, THE REST OF US WILL BE ABLE TO STICK AROUND AND KEEP AN EYE ON SUNNYVIEW ELEMENTARY.

AND PROTECT IT FROM EVIL!

"After the holiday weekend, we'll have another Superpet meeting," added the Great Gecko. "Then you guys can tell us all about your adventures!"

"I can't wait for one of Principal Brickford's special salads," said Boss Bunny happily.

The Superpets all laughed and talked about what excitement might await them. Turbo played along, but for some reason he couldn't quite put a paw on, he felt a little nervous.

3

AND THE WINNER IS . . .

The next morning, pretty much every single kid in Classroom C stood in a line in front of their teacher's desk. One by one they handed their permission slips to Ms. Beasley, who wrote each name on a piece of paper that she then dropped into a hat.

Turbo knew he was popular, but

he didn't think *everyone* would want to take him home for the weekend! It was nice to be so loved, though Turbo hadn't managed to shake the slight nervousness he was feeling.

Turbo thought back to some of the other times he had gone home with students of Classroom C.

That kid Eugene had been pretty nice, but Turbo had a strange feeling that Eugene suspected that Turbo wasn't just an ordinary hamster. And he couldn't let anyone find out the truth.

One time Turbo had gone home with a girl named Sally, but she woke up *way* too early. Which would have been fine, but she woke Turbo up with her. A hamster had to get his beauty sleep!

Then there was the time Turbo had gone home with this kid named Charlie. Charlie was obsessed with cheese. Like, really obsessed. Turbo liked cheese as much as the next hamster, but not for three meals a day! It had taken all week for Turbo to get the cheesy smell out of his fur!

All of the permission slips were handed in. The kids of Classroom C were practically shaking in their seats with excitement. Ms. Beasley said a few words about responsibility and what an honor this was and *blah blah blah*, but all Turbo could hear was his own heart beating. The suspense!

Ms. Beasley reached into the hat, pulled out a crumpled piece of paper, and read out a name.

"Yes!" yelled Meredith, a tall girl wearing pink, in the front of the classroom.

"Noooooooooooooooooooooooo!" screamed a voice from the back of the classroom.

Turbo turned to see who it was. It was that kid, Eugene. He seemed really upset that Meredith had won, but Turbo wasn't sure why. Meredith seemed perfectly fine to him.

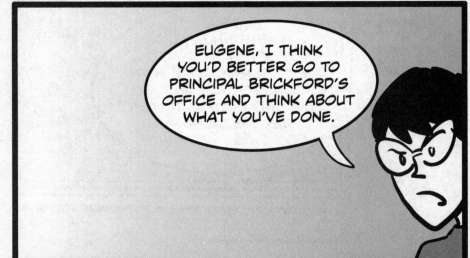

"But—but—" Eugene stammered.

Ms. Beasley raised an eyebrow.

Eugene dropped his head, closed his books, and walked to the front of the class. As he passed Turbo's cage, Eugene quickly stuffed a piece of paper through the wire. A secret note!

While everyone was paying atten-
tion to the front of the class, Turbo
unrolled the note.

Who was Little
Miss Stinky Pinky?
Who was Cap-
tain Awesome?
And what on
earth was all
this about evil
feet? Suddenly, a
shadow fell over
his cage.

Turbo looked up to see the smiling
face of Meredith.

"Hey, Turbo!" she said with a grin.
"This weekend you're going to be
mine. All mine!"

4

WHAT'S FAT AND FUZZY?

Before Turbo could believe it, the weekend arrived. He found himself in the car on the way to Meredith's house. All week Turbo had tried to tell himself things would be fine. But Eugene's warning had made him nervous. What kind of evil might await him at Meredith's house?

Turbo peeked under his food bowl. *Phew*, he thought. His super cape and goggles were still safely tucked under there. Well, no matter what sort of dangers awaited him, he'd be ready to face them as Super Turbo!

The car pulled to a stop and Meredith picked up Turbo's cage.

Turbo ran to the bars of his cage for a look, but all he could see was the back of Meredith's mom. Meredith carried him up the stairs, two at a time, to her bedroom.

"And this is where you'll be staying!" she said, plunking him down on top of a dresser. "Now just you wait here!" said Meredith excitedly.

"Because there's someone you have to meet!" She ran from the room and Turbo looked around.

The wall, the carpet, the bedspread, the pillows . . . every single thing in Meredith's entire bedroom was pink!

So this is what Eugene had meant by Little Miss Stinky *Pinky*. Clearly Eugene wasn't a fan of the color

pink, but Turbo didn't have a problem with it. After all, his cute little nose and his ears were pink!

Turbo sniffed the air. "It even *smells* pink in here! Pink and . . . something else. Something fuzzy. . . ."

Suddenly, Meredith came running back in, carrying that something.

ZOOEY! MEET TURBO!
TURBO, THIS IS ZOOEY!

Meredith held up the biggest, fattest, fuzziest cat Turbo had ever seen! This cat was bigger than, like, six Wonder Pigs.

The cat was also, as far as Turbo could tell, fast asleep. Which suited Turbo just fine. He was a pretty brave hamster, but maybe a little less brave when it came to cats who were so big they could eat him in one gulp!

Meredith dumped Zooey onto her bed and picked up an even bigger, fuzzier something.

AND THIS LITTLE GIRL IS FRANNY!

This cat was like a Zooey *plus* a Wonder Pig.

Franny lazily opened one yellow eye and peered at Turbo. Turbo gulped. Meredith plopped Franny onto the bed next to Zooey.

"I'm so excited you're staying here with us!" said Meredith, petting her cats. "You, me, Franny, and Zooey are going to have the best time together."

Turbo let out a little squeak.

From the bed, Franny looked up
at him, yawned, and licked her lips.

EYE SEE YOU!

For the next hour, Meredith, Franny, Zooey, and Turbo all played together in her bedroom. Just kidding.

For the next hour, Meredith baby-talked to the two cats while they slept. Meredith was tying big pink ribbons on everybody—one on Zooey's head, another around Franny's tail, and a

big frilly bow right around Turbo's
middle.

No matter what Meredith did to
the cats, they both remained asleep.

And thank goodness for that! Turbo had caught a glimpse of Zooey's fangs when she yawned earlier.

You just can't trust anything with fangs like that! Turbo thought to himself. *Still, it's strange that they nap so much. It's almost like they're saving their energy for something. . . .*

Meredith closed the door behind her and hauled the two sleepy cats off to dinner. Now that he was alone in the room, Turbo let out the deep breath he'd been holding.

He spent a few minutes surveying the room. He could either take this time to relax or . . . he could explore! He decided to take a chance while Meredith and the cats were at dinner and see what he was working with.

He peered over the edge of his cage. *Boy, I really am up high,* he thought. *Maybe too high for a normal hamster to get down from.* . . . Turbo smiled to himself.

The bedspread was so cushy, Super Turbo struggled to get up. When he finally managed it, he decided to have himself a little super adventure.

SUPER TURBO BATTLED THE FLUFFY PINK BEAR OF DESPAIR!

SUPER TURBO MET HIS EVIL MIRROR-IMAGE SELF, OBRUT REPUS!

Super Turbo fell back, gasping! There was a big, round, yellow eye staring at him from under the door! He'd been spotted!

As quickly as he could, Super Turbo scrambled back up to his cage. He hid his cape and goggles just as Meredith swung open the door, carrying Franny and Zooey, each cat tucked under an arm. They looked sound asleep. But if they were asleep, then who had been peeking under the door at Turbo?

When Meredith's mother finally yelled for Meredith to go to bed, Super Turbo was relieved. Hopefully, he could get some rest now too.

For the first time, Franny and Zooey moved by themselves. Zooey stretched out next to Meredith's head and Franny curled up near her feet.

Turbo hadn't expected that the cats would be sleeping in the room with them. *Good thing my cage is up so high!* he thought. And before he knew it, he was fast asleep.

⑥

HIDE AND GO EEEEEK

Turbo woke up to a strange noise. For a second, he forgot where he was. Then he saw two round, glowing eyes staring at him in the darkness.

"AAAH!" he yelled.

"Interesssting cossstume you had on before," a voice purred from the darkness. "What are you? A superhero?"

It must be one of the cats! thought Turbo. *The one who saw me under the door! But which one?*

"Who— who's there?" asked Turbo, trying his best to sound brave.

"Oh, it's jussssst me," said the voice. "Franny."

Turbo heard his cage creak and he could tell that Franny was sitting *on* it.

"So what are you? A superhero?"
Franny repeated.

Now that his vision was getting
used to the darkness, Turbo could
see her looming above him.

TEEHEEHEE . . .

SUPER TURBO! I THINK YOU SHOULD COME OUT OF YOUR CAGE NOW, SUPER TURBO.

UH, WHY?

BECAUSE I'VE BEEN SLEEPING ALL DAY AND NOW IT'S TIME TO PLAY HIDE-AND-SEEK.

"Um, no, I don't think so," said Turbo, gathering up his courage. "It's late, it's dark, and I'm tired. I don't feel like playing. I'll play with you tomorrow."

"Tomorrow I'll be tired." Franny yawned, showing off her mouthful of very large, very sharp white teeth. "I want to play now."

Turbo suddenly realized that he was *in* his hamster cage, and Franny was *outside* it. He was perfectly safe! He puffed out his chest. "No, Franny," he said firmly.

Then Turbo watched in horror as Franny's paw reached down, and with a flick of a claw, popped open the cage door.

"Hide-and-seek. I'm going

to count to ten, and then I'll come get you," Franny said with a purr.

Above him, Turbo could hear Franny start counting. He'd been in some tight spots before, but nothing quite like this. He glanced over at where he kept his cape and goggles. He reached for them.

"... nine, ten!" Franny finished counting. "Ready or not, here I come."

Franny reached her paw into Turbo's cage. It got closer and closer ... and closer! And then, at the last possible second, Super Turbo bolted out the door of his cage as fast as he could. He grabbed his pink ribbon and used it to swing off the dresser and onto the floor.

As soon as Super Turbo hit the ground, he started running as fast as his hamster feet could carry him. He had to get out of there!

7

ON THE RUN!

Super Turbo was exhausted. He'd spent the entire night darting from one hiding place to another. Truthfully, he hadn't actually *seen* Franny the cat since he'd escaped, but you can never be too careful. Especially when you're hiding from a giant cat!

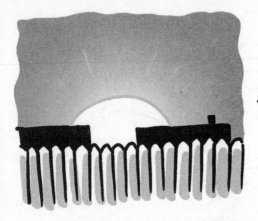

The sun was just starting to come up and Super Turbo could hardly keep his eyes open. Now that he could see a little better, Super Turbo knew he *had* to find a place to rest. "Just for a minute, only a minute," he muttered to himself sleepily.

Super Turbo noticed the bookshelf just then. It reminded him of his own cozy little book nook in Classroom C. Oh, how he wished he were there now!

More tired than he'd ever felt, Super Turbo crawled into a little space between two books that were leaning against each other. He thought of his friends back at Sunnyview

Elementary. Would he ever see them again? Would they ever know what happened to their pal Super Turbo? He pulled up his goggles and wiped a small tear from his eye.

GREAT GECKO, SO BRAVE!

GREEN WINGER AND FANTASTIC FISH, SUCH GOOD FRIENDS!

PROFESSOR TURTLE, SO SMART!

SCIENCE NEWS

PENELOPE, SO CAMOUFLAGED—
AND SO IN NEED OF A
SUPERHERO NAME!

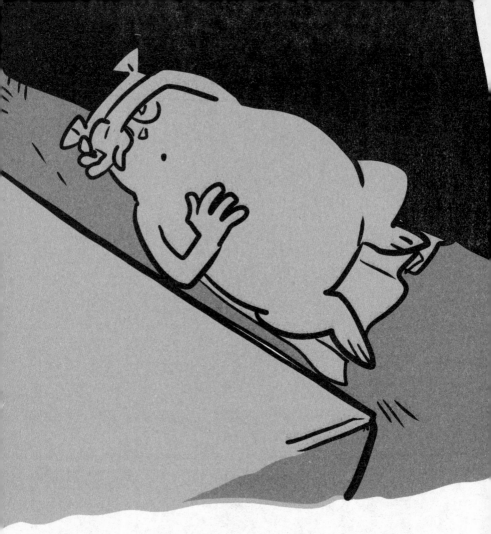

And with that thought, Super
Turbo fell asleep.

Super Turbo had many strange dreams. He dreamed of Classroom C and all his friends. He dreamed of pinkness, pinkness as far as the eye could see. He dreamed he heard loud footsteps, and voices calling

his name. He dreamed he heard someone crying. And he dreamed of sharp white teeth and two huge yellow eyes. . . .

Oh wait, he wasn't dreaming. Two huge yellow eyes were staring right at him.

He was caught! Was this the end for Super Turbo?!

8

HINT: IT'S NOT THE END

A huge, whiskered snout squeezed into the space between the two books where Super Turbo had been hiding. It sniffed. Super Turbo backed up as far as he could. He closed his eyes and threw his arms over his face.

"It's Zooey," said the snout.

A second passed, then two. Super Turbo slowly opened his eyes.

"It's Zooey," the snout repeated.

Turbo was confused "Uh . . . hi?" he said.

Zooey's face suddenly spread into a huge smile. "Boy, am I glad I found

you!" he said. "But not as happy as Franny will be! Hey, Franny! I found him!"

Super Turbo leaped forward, waving his paws. "No, wait! *Shhh*! Don't tell—"

"Oh, thank goodness you're okay!" yelled Franny, bounding into view. She rubbed her giant cat head against Super Turbo's whole body.

"Okay? Okay
I am? I am
okay?" Super
Turbo repeated,
trying to understand what Franny
had just said.

WE WERE LOOKING
FOR YOU ALL NIGHT.
WE HAD NO IDEA
WHERE YOU'D GONE!

YOU KNOW, I AM PRETTY HUNGRY. . . .

SHE EATS, LIKE, WAY MORE THAN ME.

CAN WE GET OUT OF HERE?

"Of course!" said Franny happily. "Come on, we have to let Meredith and her family know you're okay!"

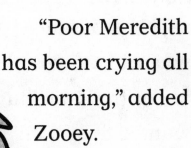

"Poor Meredith has been crying all morning," added Zooey.

"So last night, when you were reaching into my cage," said Super

Turbo, "what were you doing if you weren't trying to eat me?"

Franny looked shocked. "I told you! I just wanted to play! You looked like you were having so much fun in your superhero suit when I saw you under the door that I wanted to join in!"

"Well, why didn't you join in earlier?" asked Turbo "Why did you wait until the middle of the night?"

Franny laughed as if Super Turbo

were a
hilarious
little hamster.
"I couldn't
let Meredith
see you in your
superhero outfit, silly,"
she said.

Turbo had to admit, she had a great point.

"Now let's get you back in your cage before Meredith comes back in here," said Franny. "You've got to hide your superhero suit. We can't let your secret out!"

AND WITH THAT, THE CATS KINDLY HELPED SUPER TURBO BACK INTO HIS CAGE.

Turbo
tucked
his super
gear safely
away just
as Meredith
came back into
the room. It did look like she had
been crying.

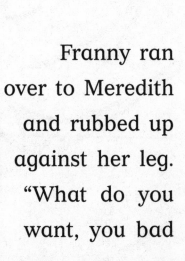

Franny ran
over to Meredith
and rubbed up
against her leg.
"What do you
want, you bad

kitt—TURBO! You're all right!" Meredith cried when she saw him safe in his cage.

Meredith scooped up Turbo and hugged him so tight that he saw stars. Turbo looked over her shoulder at Franny and Zooey, who gave him a paws-up. Turbo knew his secret was safe with them.

9

HOME AT LAST!

"And that's how I spent my long weekend!" Super Turbo looked out at the rest of the Superpet Superhero League. They were sitting all around him in the familiar old book nook in the corner of Classroom C.

"That was *some* adventure, Super Turbo!" said the Green Winger with

a whistle. "I just hung around in the sun!"

"Yeah, my weekend was nothing like that!" added Wonder Pig. "Although I did find a nickel."

"And your story was just one day!" said the Great Gecko. "What happened the rest of the weekend?"

"Lots of hide-and-seek with my

new friends," Super Turbo said with
a laugh. "How were things at the

school?" he asked the pets who had
remained there.

PRETTY QUIET,
I GUESS.

YEAH. ALTHOUGH
WE DID HAVE THIS
ENORMOUS BATTLE
WITH WHISKERFACE
AND HIS RAT PACK.

Later that night, Super Turbo took off his cape and goggles and hid them in their secret spot. There was already something in the secret spot, though—a piece of catnip Franny and

Zooey had given him so he'd never forget them. Well, at least not until the catnip disintegrated.

Turbo was happy the cats hadn't turned out to be evil, but he was even happier to be back with his friends and members of the mighty Superpet Superhero League!